How Hanukkah Saved C...

by

Doreen Lawrence

Elisha Vision Publishing

This book is available through:

Elisha Vision Publishing

PO Box 1601

Wake Forest, NC 27588

Or it can be ordered directly from www.ElishaVision.com

This book was printed in the USA by

InstantPublisher.com
P.O. Box 340, 410 Highway 72 W.
Collierville TN 38027

ISBN 978-0-9843958-1-1

DEDICATION

I would like to dedicate this book to all of my grandchildren: Alyssa, Kai, Canyon, Roan, Alyson, Oscar, and any new little ones to come in the future as God allows. My prayer is that they, as well as your children, will be blessed with a relationship with Jesus that will take them through anything they face, and may His Light shine through them to the world.

Acknowledgements

I wish to thank all who have encouraged me in the writing of this book. There have been way too many to mention by name.

When John Fisk, our dear friend and co-minister, preached a sermon by the title, "How Hanukkah Saved Christmas," I said that there should be a children's book by that name. John and his wife, Sara Jean immediately encouraged me to write one. Then it was with the inspiration of my husband, Les, our three daughters and their families that the story unfolded.

It goes without saying (but must be said!) that there would be no story to tell without the grace, love, and power of Jehovah God, and His Son Jesus, by His Holy Spirit.

Dear Parents,

This is a fictional story written about fictional characters. The setting and the background, however, are inspired by our own family tradition which has developed over the years. Our grown children and their families all meet together with us at Roan Mountain State Park in Tennessee every other year for an old fashioned family Christmas celebration. We are also privileged to celebrate Hanukkah while there since the two holidays frequently coincide. My husband shares with our grandchildren about Hanukkah in much the same way as Grampa does in this story. Photographs in this book were taken from our own family vacation.

Les and I grew up understanding the true meaning of Christmas, and we still love to take advantage of the opportunity to celebrate the miraculous birth of our Savior. We did not understand Hanukkah, however until we were grown with families of our own. Understanding how the two seasons relate has become very important to us since our understanding of our

Hebrew roots has grown and developed. Jewish history is also OUR history. Our Messiah is also THEIR Messiah. We share a common bond which is eternal.

My prayer is that this book becomes a teaching tool for you to teach your children the importance of our roots in Judaism. God's plan is eternal. It began in Genesis and continues today. It is fulfilled in Yeshua, the Jewish Messiah. May you and your family be blessed during this wonderful season of the year.

Doreen Lawrence

Chapter One

Last Day of School

Matt and Rachel grabbed the bars of the trapeze swings at the playground outside their Savannah middle school, and effortlessly swung their legs through their arms and over the bars. December in Georgia had occasional days that seemed more like summer than winter. This was one of them. They sat up and began swinging as they had done a thousand times before. Sometimes it seemed that these two close friends spent half their lives on these trapeze swings. Rachel, a petite blonde, preferred anything athletic over girl stuff. She was totally at home on these swings with her best friend, Matt. He was really more like a brother than just a neighbor. They were discussing what they would be doing in the coming week. This was the last day of school before winter vacation. Both twelve year olds were excited to finally be out of school, if only for a couple of weeks. They would only have to spend two more hours in the classroom after lunch, and then they would be out. Matt and Rachel had been best friends as well as neighbors ever since Rachel's family moved next door six years before. Rachel was more quiet than usual on this sunny afternoon, but Matt, bubbling over with excitement, almost fell off his trapeze!

"This is going to be the best Christmas ever," exclaimed Matt. "We are going to the mountains in Tennessee and all of our aunts and uncles and cousins and grandparents are coming. We are staying in cabins next to each other. We go and cut down a real Christmas tree and everything. We get to make our own decorations, and we'll probably even get to play in the snow! At least it usually snows up there at Christmas. I can't wait. We are packing up tonight and leaving tomorrow. We are taking loads of presents. We'll come back a couple of days after Christmas. Then we will have a few days when you and I can play together. I'll call you when we get back." Matt was talking so fast that he hardly took a breath as he let his story spill out.

"How nice for you," retorted a slightly dejected Rachel. She sounded angry.

"What's wrong with you?" asked Matt, noticing for the first time that Rachel wasn't her normal chatty self.

"We don't celebrate Christmas. We celebrate Hanukkah

in my religion, and it is already past. I'm not even all that excited about vacation. I got some neat Hanukkah presents, though - a new computer and games. I suppose it'll be okay."

"What is Hanukkah, anyway? I've never heard much about it. And why don't Jews celebrate Christmas?" asked Matt. Holding tightly to the chains, they swung their feet over their heads, let go, and landed simultaneously with a "THUMP" onto the gravel.

Rachel took a deep breath and told her story as though she had said it a hundred times and this was just one more. "Well, a couple of thousand years ago Israel was invaded by enemies. They were destroying the land and even came and messed up the Temple in Jerusalem where the people worshipped God. They put disgusting things on the altar and stole stuff and everything. Then a guy named Judas Maccabeus came in with his army and drove out the enemy and cleaned up the Temple so the people could worship God again. When the people lit the Temple lamps, there was only enough oil for one day, but it stayed lit for eight days until they could get more oil. It was a real miracle and we celebrate the miracle of the lights. That is why we light eight candles. We light one candle for each of the eight days that the lamps stayed lit. That's also why we have gifts on all eight days. We don't celebrate Christmas because that's Christian, and we are not Christian." She spoke this last statement with finality, in the same tone she heard her parents use whenever she asked them the same question.

"I can't imagine still celebrating something that happened so long ago." said Matt with disdain.

"Well, Christmas happened 2000 years ago! And you celebrate it!"

"Yeah, but that was the birth of the Son of God! A little more important than cleaning house, I think!"

"That's your opinion!" Rachel shot back, tossing her long blond ponytail for emphasis. She was offended but didn't really have an answer for Matt's retort. She always shied away from the superiority that Christian kids seemed to have. Rachel's family was not particularly religious, so she didn't understand the differences that kept them apart. Christmas was definitely not her favorite time of year and especially not her favorite subject. She always felt left out during this festive time. Hopefully things would get back to normal after the New Year.

The shrill sound of the school bell startled them both out of their discussion. Matt and Rachel discovered new meaning for the phrase, "Saved by the bell." For a change, both were relieved to be called back into the classroom. At least this uncomfortable conversation could end.

Chapter Two

Headed to the Mountains

Matt's Mom hustled about getting things ready to go to the mountains. She had her hands full as she carried things out to the van. Looking around for some help, she said, "Matt, get that box over there and bring it out to me, please. It needs to go in before the rest of this stuff." The plan was to get everything packed into the van tonight so they could leave early the next morning for the long drive to the Blue Ridge Mountains where their cabins awaited them. "It seems that we take more stuff with us every time we do this trip!" his Mom muttered as she stumbled through the pile of boxes and suitcases. When she tripped and almost fell into the pillows and blankets, Matt could hardly keep himself from laughing.

"I saw that!" exclaimed his mother with mock sternness. "Don't even THINK of laughing at me!" With this she threw the blankets at Matt and he fell over himself. This time he and she both broke into peals of laughter. The anticipation of a week in the mountains had put them both in a great mood.

As his Mom continued with her task, Matt

wandered into his room and started thinking about the trip. Their Christmas family reunion had been taking place every two years since Matt could remember. They had spent Christmas every other year at Roan Mountain State Park in the Blue Ridge Mountains of Tennessee. The odd year was usually spent at home or at the other grandparent's house. They took everything from clothing to groceries to craft materials and Christmas presents. Matt was glad that all he had to think about was his small suitcase. He fell back on the bed and thought about the next day and all the fun they would have. He also thought back on his conversation with Rachel. He sort of felt sorry for her to be missing out on all this fun. Hanukkah sounded like a boring celebration to him, especially compared to Christmas. Sure, she got presents for 8 days in a row, but they had no Christmas tree and no Christmas carols. The Jewish people seemed to miss out on so much...

Still daydreaming, Matt heard a yell from the driveway. "I'm still waiting for that box! Matt! What ARE you doing?!"

"Nothing, I'm just..."

"WHA...." His Mom's voice was sounding incredulous.

"I mean, I'm pa-packing my suitcase," Matt stuttered as he jerked himself into action and quickly opened the still empty case. One thing he did not need to confess to Mom was that he actually was doing...NOTHING! "I'm sorry, Mom. Here it is." Matt carried the big box outside. What's in it, anyway?"

"That's for you to find out on Christmas Day!" Mom's voice had softened and her smile had returned.

"Cool!" A repentant Matt exclaimed as he started back to his own room.

"Hold on there, young man. I'm not through with you yet! You need to go to the van and make sure it is cleaned out. I think your gym bag is still there and your backpack. You won't need those unless you plan to do some homework," she suggested with a twinkle. "And we definitely don't need your gym clothes to sit in the car all week! "Phew!" She added as she made a wrinkly face and held her nose.

"Yes, Ma'am," Matt grumbled. He went outside to the van and did as his mother had asked. Homework definitely did not belong on this trip! He did not intend to learn anything new! Except maybe what was in that box...

Chapter Three

A New Friend?

Matt's dad was always anxious to get an early start, so they were on the road well before dawn. After several hours of travel, Matt's family arrived first and got everything unloaded. Being an only child, Matt was very glad to see that another family was also moving in to a cabin a few doors down. A boy, looking to be about Matt's age, was with them. Since shyness was never a problem for Matt, he went over and introduced himself. The boy's name was Ryan, and he was 11 years old - only a few months younger than Matt. They had a lot of fun playing around the grounds. They went down to the creek and threw stones into the icy water and talked of how much fun it would be to come back and rock hop when the weather was warmer. It was amazing how much colder it was here than in Georgia. Ryan was from Georgia too, so he also noticed a big difference in the weather. They both were hoping for snow so they could slide down the nearby hill. What good was it to be cold if there was no snow? The two boys started back across the field toward the cabins.

"Hey, Matt, look over there!" Ryan exclaimed as he pointed to a tree across the meadow. Just as Matt turned to look, Ryan stuck his foot in front of Matt and Matt went sprawling. Ryan laughed as though this was the funniest thing he had ever seen. "What did you do that for?" yelled Matt as he struggled to his feet and brushed the grass off of his clothes. "That was really stupid!"

"Hey, what's the matter? That was funny. Can't you take a joke?" Ryan retorted.

"Some joke. I bet you wouldn't be laughing if I did it to you!"

"Sure I would. I know something funny when I see it. Even when the joke is on me." Ryan stuck his chest out and swaggered back to Matt's side.

"Yeah, right!" Somehow Matt didn't quite believe him.

After an hour of playing outside, Matt took

Ryan to his cabin where his Mom was already baking cookies and Dad was lighting a fire in the fireplace. The firewood and kindling were stacked up high and ready for a long evening. The cousins still had not arrived, so Matt was content to play with his new friend, even if he was a bit strange.

"Mom and Dad, this is Ryan. His family is staying a couple of cabins down. May we paint Christmas tree decorations?"

Mom considered this question for a moment and then answered, "I was planning on saving that for later, but I guess it will be ok. Just please make sure you keep the table neat and clean. We are all having dinner here later when the others arrive. Here's a plate of chocolate chip cookies, boys. I imagine you will figure out what to do with them." Mom set the plate down in the middle of the table and handed the boys the paints and plaster decorations. She also carefully placed paper toweling under their work to keep everything clean.

As the boys painted, Matt opened up the conversation. "Have you ever heard of Hanukkah?" he asked Ryan.

"Not really."

"Oh. I have a friend that celebrates Hanukkah instead of Christmas."

"So what?"

"Nothing. I just wondered if you knew anything about it."

"Yeah, well I don't."

Matt decided to change the subject.

Things went okay for about an hour. The boys painted quietly and talked about themselves and got to know each other. Matt was actually quite good at painting. He had always loved art and anything that had to do with drawing or painting. His ornament was looking very good but Ryan was having a difficult time with his. He was not very patient, and he was much better playing outside games than he was at painting a delicate Christmas ornament. This was actually the first time he had even tried anything like this.

"Look, Ryan," Matt suggested, "Just put a little dot of red right there and..."

"Ughhh!" yelled Ryan in frustration. "I can't do this stuff! It's girl stuff! I'm going home!" With this exclamation, Ryan picked up the red paint and threw it down hard, spattering paint on the cookies and the table. The wall, chairs and floor also felt Ryan's wrath when he picked up the green paint and tossed it, bouncing it off the wall and splashing it everywhere.   With that, Ryan stormed out the door which he slammed firmly behind him.

Matt and his Mom stared after Ryan, not knowing how to react to this act of violence. Needless to say, Matt was horrified and somehow felt that it was his fault. Mom was flabbergasted by the uncontrollable behavior and the awful mess that was left for them to clean up. Trying not to lose her own temper, she held her tongue for a moment. Matt was frozen in his chair dreading what would come next.

"Matt, throw the cookies away." Mom instructed quietly through gritted teeth. "And start cleaning up the paint before it dries. We can't eat dinner until all this is cleaned up with soap and water." She spat out each word one by one as she gestured broadly towards the dining area of the cabin.

"But Mom! Why do I have to..."

"Matt. Just do it."

"Ok, Mom. But why do we have to throw away the cookies? Some of them may not have been spattered. I only ate one!"

"They may have paint on them that we can't see. Even though it is not considered toxic paint, I don't believe it was meant to be eaten. Throw them away. I can make more."

"Yes, Mom," Matt said dejectedly as he began the monumental job. Then under his breath he said, "I wish Judas Maccabeus was here." He was remembering Rachel's story about the mess he had to clean up.

"What did you say?"

"Oh, nothing," mumbled Matt, thinking that cleaning the mess in the Jewish temple was certainly worse than this.

Chapter Four

Reunion

Later that evening, after the flurry of greetings of cousins and other relatives, the entire family sat around at a dinner of lasagna and all the trimmings. They had already gone through the "My, how you've grown!" comments and the kisses and hugs from the adults. Matt and his cousins, fourteen year old Nathan, nine year old Anna, six year old Tyler, and the baby Emma, who was one, greeted one another enthusiastically.   Nathan was Matt's hero, since he was the oldest boy of the group, and very athletic.   Nathan was everything Matt wanted to be, and he admired him openly.   Nate, Matt, and Anna, who was a tomboy, had always been inseparable. Poor Tyler tried to keep up with the others, but most of the time he was left hopelessly in the dust. Emma was content to simply stay with her mama and out of the way of the older members of the tribe.

Grampa was also a favorite of Matt's. He always seemed to know about interesting things. He was a big sports fan, so he was always up to date on the games of the season, whether it was basketball, football, or whatever. He also loved to get out and play with the kids at whatever activity they wanted. They would go for long walks in the woods and down by the stream. They would look at things in nature and he would explain them. Whenever there was snow, he would always slide with them. Grampa was just cool, that's all. Matt's friends were kind of nervous around him because he was a preacher, but Matt couldn't understand the problem. Grampa wasn't at all stuffy or formal or judgmental like the kids expected. Instead, he just really seemed to understand God. Like he knew Him personally. Like they were friends, or something. Something inside of Matt wanted to know God like that.

"So, Matt, how is everything going with you?' asked Grampa, as he reached for another piece of garlic bread.

"Fine," was his short reply.

"I heard you had a little excitement today."

"Yeah, I guess. I met a new kid, Ryan. At first he was fun and cool, but he has a strange sense of humor and a real temper. He made an awful mess and I had to clean it all up."

"Wow, bummer. Doesn't sound like much of a friend."

"Right. That's the truth. I wish Rachel was here. She's a REAL friend."

"Rachel? I met her, didn't I?"

"Yes, Grampa. She goes to school with me and lives in my neighborhood. Her family is Jewish and she doesn't celebrate Christmas. She celebrates Hanukkah," Matt said as he rolled his eyes scornfully.

"Oh, really. That's interesting." Grampa responded thoughtfully. He made a mental note to pursue this conversation further at another time.

Chapter Five

Christmas Eve

The first full day at Roan Mountain was spent getting the Christmas tree and setting it up in one of the cabins. The decision was made to put it in the middle cabin, which was where Nathan and Anna's family stayed. The men and older kids went to get the tree and they got the biggest tree they could find! In fact, it was the biggest

Christmas tree they had EVER seen! (Except the one in Rockefeller Plaza, maybe!) It was so tall that it touched the high ceiling and so fat that it took up half the room! All the moms laughed at the men for getting it so big. All the furniture had to be moved around to make room for it and it took all day to make paper chains and home made ornaments to decorate it. They even strung popcorn with needles and thread. There was popcorn everywhere! At least it was a lot more fun to clean up than Ryan's mess. Everyone did it together, and it actually became part of the celebration. The day ended with the family all gathering together to play games. Matt, Nate and Anna went up to the loft to hang out and catch up on each other's lives. Everyone left late and returned to his own cabin for the night. The next morning Matt came downstairs long after his usual time.

"Morning, Matt. So you decided to get up!" Quipped his father.

"Morning." Matt was not given to much conversation in the morning and was still half asleep.

"Could you get me some more firewood? It's just outside the door."

"Yeah, okay." Matt went to the door and began to step outside. He skipped, skidded and slid into the porch rocker and exclaimed, "Whoa, what the..!"

"What's going on out there?" his dad asked.

"There's a huge rat just outside our door! I almost stepped on it. Aagh," Matt shivered at the very thought. "How disgusting!"

"Who would do such a thing?" asked his father.

"There's only one person I can think of who has that kind of warped sense of humor. Ryan. He has done some weird stuff since we got here. I don't trust him. I didn't see him all day yesterday because we were so busy with the tree. I bet he was jealous or something."

"He's alone, isn't he? I mean, no other kids here with his group."

"Yeah. He's probably bored stiff."

As the day's activities got underway, the whole episode was soon forgotten. Unnoticed, Dad quietly disposed of the unfortunate rodent.

That night was Christmas Eve. The family tradition for this night was to come together for the evening meal and then go throughout the campground Christmas caroling. After this, everyone would go into the cabin, sit around the tree, and listen to the Christmas story from the Bible. It was usually Grampa who read and talked about the Christmas story.

"So, children, what is Christmas REALLY about?" Grampa began.

"Presents!" Tyler piped up.

Anna said, "No, Tyler, it's Jesus' birthday!"

"Yes, but WE get to keep His birthday presents!" Tyler was rather proud of his cleverness and knew he was being naughty.

Grampa commented thoughtfully, "Maybe Jesus will decide to do something else with His birthday presents. I think one little boy is getting a bit full of himself." Grampa tried to look stern, but no one bought it.

"I'm sorry, Grampa. I'm just really excited."

"I know, Tyler. But lets think about Jesus now. Not new toys."

"Oookaay." Tyler climbed into Grampa's lap and snuggled in for the story.

The other children snickered at Tyler's antics. Quickly, however, they sobered and sat up ready to hear the wonderful report of that extraordinary night in Bethlehem when a young woman gave birth to the Son of God in a stable where animals lived. It truly was a story that would never get old. Stars shone in each of their eyes at the thought of the great shining star that announced the place where Jesus was born. They imagined what it would have been like to hear the angels from Heaven make that wonderful declaration! How surprised the shepherds must have been to see and hear this amazing thing!

"For there is born to you this day in the city of David a Savior, who is Christ the Lord. And this will be the sign to you: You will find a Babe wrapped in swaddling cloths, lying in a manger." Grampa read the verses from the book of Luke with great feeling, as though it was the first time he had ever read it. Parents and children alike were transfixed with these words from the greatest story ever told.

Grampa finished reading the Bible account and continued speaking. "It is all true, you know. This really happened 2000 years ago in a town that still exists today. I have walked on the streets of Bethlehem. I have seen the fields where the shepherds stood that night so long ago. I have walked on the streets of Jerusalem where Jesus frequently went.

"You were there, Grampa?" asked Anna.

"Yes, I went with a tour group a few years ago...I wasn't actually there when Jesus was! I know you think I'm ancient but I'm not that old!" Grampa added in mocked offense.

"I didn't mean that, Grampa!" A red blush crept up on poor Anna's face as the whole family laughed.

"Getting back to the story..." continued Grampa. "Seeing the land of Israel was wonderful. I hope you can all go sometime. It is the same land where Jesus lived and had His ministry. It is still God's chosen land.

"Don't consider this just another tale. This is the story of life itself. This is the story of God's love for us.   Don't ever forget or underestimate the power of it all. God gave His Son so that we could have life.   This is the greatest gift of all. Tomorrow, when we all gather under this MAMMOTH Christmas tree..." Grampa paused as each one looked up and smiled at the brightly lit tree which could not be ignored, .."We must not forget why we have the privilege of being here at all. It's because of Him. Remember Jesus. He wants to be a part of our celebration."

"Okay, Grampa, we will," said Matt soberly. "I really feel as though this Christmas is different, somehow.   I don't know why, I just...and...I can't seem to get Hanukkah out of my mind - or my friend Rachel, back home."

"It's all right, Matt, I understand. We will talk some more later. I think there are a few things you will find interesting." Grampa had a knowing look as he closed the Bible and set it on the coffee table.

Everyone in the room looked curiously at Grampa and Matt and wondered what they were talking about, but no one asked questions. "We'll know soon enough," they thought, "But tomorrow's CHRISTMAS!" It was time for bed.

Later, as Matt was laying in bed thinking about the day, he realized that one thing had been missing this week. He really had hoped that it would snow. He was disappointed for a moment, and then remembered that he could pray. He knew that God could give them snow if He wanted to. So Matt prayed, "Lord, if it would be okay with you, could it please snow while we are here?" He rolled over and went to sleep, dreaming of sledding and flying snowballs.

Chapter Six

A Special Christmas Gift

Matt was the first to awaken on Christmas morning. Because they were tucked away between the mountains, the sunrise came late. Even though it was already after 8 o'clock, the sun was just now beginning to light up the sky. Matt got out of bed and looked out the window. He gasped in delight as he saw the sparkle of new fallen snow that graced every surface with unbroken, unspoiled white. Remembering his prayer the night before, Matt was filled with awe and a new sense of faith that God had answered him. Exactly. Perfectly. His Christmas was already complete and he hadn't even opened the first gift from under the tree. And somehow, it wasn't even about the snow. It was the fact that God had taken notice of him and heard his prayer. Matt knew without a doubt that it had snowed just for him last night. God loved him that much.

Jumping up from the window, Matt ran downstairs from his little loft bedroom and woke his parents. They all dressed as quickly as possible and ran outside to make the first imprint on that beautiful white expanse. The others emerged from their cabins at the same time and sledding actually became a priority over opening the Christmas presents.

Two hours and many cups of hot chocolate later, they all did gather around the tree and joyfully received the gifts from each other. Everyone got exactly what they wanted...and more. What a wonderful day it turned out to be! After dinner the kids all dressed again in their warm clothes and went out to slide some more.

For the first time since Ryan exploded at the table in his cabin, Matt saw him. He was standing all alone, leaning against a tree and kicking at the snow with his toe.

Matt approached him and said, "Merry Christmas, Ryan."

"Yeah, whatever."

Ryan started to walk away, but Matt could see that he didn't want to go. He had a very guilty look on his face, but was stubbornly hanging on to his pride. At that very moment, Matt had an idea.

"Ryan, I'm sorry I haven't played with you for the past couple of days."

Ryan swung around with an amazed look on his face. "You're sorry? I'm the one who did all the nasty stuff to you. And.. the rat... that was me too. I'm sorry, Matt." Ryan looked down at his feet and resumed poking his toe into the snow.

"I forgive you, Ryan.   This day is too wonderful to be mad!" Matt was still basking in the glow of the love that he felt from God answering his prayer about the snow.

Matt introduced Ryan to his cousins and they all had a good time together the rest of the day.   It made Matt feel good inside to have a chance to forgive Ryan and be a friend to him. Yes, this was a very special Christmas.

Chapter Seven

Grampa's Surprise

Only one more day. One more night. Then tomorrow everyone would load up and go back home. Matt didn't want to think about it. This Christmas had gone by so fast! They had sledded each day since Christmas, played until they had no strength left, eaten until they thought they could burst, and laughed until they hurt. Sleep was a necessity which overtook them all in their utter exhaustion. Matt leaned back on his bed and listened to the quiet. It was oh, so quiet here in the snowy mountains. Never being one to want things quiet, Matt was beginning to get used to it and appreciate it. Sleep came swiftly.

After breakfast the next morning, Grampa came in and said that everyone was to gather at his cabin after dinner that evening. He said that he had a surprise. He would not give any hints, except to say that this would be something they had never done before. There was an air of mystery about him and he had a twinkle in his eye.

"What's going on, Grampa?" Matt asked.

"You'll find out tonight. God has an interesting way of putting things together," Grampa said over his shoulder as he went down the porch steps.

As the day progressed, not another thought was given to what Grampa had said. The day was full of more play. The snow was melting and was perfect for snowball fights and constructing snowmen. About noon Ryan's family left and everyone said their goodbyes. Ryan and Matt exchanged email addresses and promised to keep in touch.

Cold and happy, Matt went back to his cabin and sat by the fire that Dad always kept burning brightly. He ate cookies and played with his Christmas toys. He especially liked the brain teaser puzzles that his folks had given him. This simple toy had been number one on his wish list. He now handled this tangle of rings, trying to figure out how to separate them. Once he got this puzzle mastered, he would go on to the next.

Being an only child, Matt had learned to be comfortable with himself and knew how to play alone. Having all of the cousins around had been fun, but this quiet play could be fun too. Nate and Anna were also in their cabin and Tyler and Emma had gone out with their parents to the store. This was a welcome lull in the activities. It gave Matt a chance to stop and think about all that had happened. Ryan turned out to be a pretty good friend after all. He did need to work on that temper, but no one's perfect! Nathan had changed some since the last time they had played together. He seemed less interested in Matt and more interested in the pretty girl that was staying on the other side of the circle. Anna was always fun. She reminded him a lot of Rachel. She was tough and could play hard. They had made a great snowman together earlier in the day. That ended with a vicious snowball fight where she really pulled her own weight. For a girl, Anna was pretty cool. It had been a wonderful Christmas and he was ready to go home. He missed Rachel and wondered what she was doing. Matt suddenly realized that he had never had a chance to talk to Grampa about Hanukkah, but decided that it didn't really matter. They would talk about it sometime. Matt slumped down on the couch and closed his eyes as he thought about these things. The warm fire, the quiet cabin, and the simple peace of it all had lulled him to sleep. The ring puzzle fell to the floor.

Chapter Eight

Grampa's Secret Revealed

Just as planned, they all went to Grampa's cabin after dinner. As everyone settled in, he called to Grammy to bring out a box. With mystery and a smile in his eyes, he pulled out a large bronze candlestick. He also pulled out some candles and matches.

The first reaction was a little disappointment in the seeming ordinariness of Grampa's surprise, but there was still some interest and curiosity. Matt asked, "What is that for?"

Grampa explained, "This is a menorah or Hanukkiah - a special candlestick used by the Jewish people to celebrate Hanukkah. We are going to light the candles tonight. I know Hanukkah this year is past, but I want to teach you all about its significance. I was very interested, Matt, in the fact that it had already come to your attention. I planned to do this before I knew any of that. It is very sad that Christians do not understand Hanukkah. Jesus Himself celebrated it, you know."

"Really?" asked Matt. "I don't remember ever seeing that word in the Bible.

"The word 'Hanukkah' isn't in the Bible," replied Grampa. "The Hanukkah celebration is referred to by different names. The Feast of Lights, and the Feast of Dedication are other names for Hanukkah. The Gospel of John says that Jesus went up to Jerusalem at the time of the Feast of Dedication. This Feast honored an event that had happened less than 200 years earlier.

All the children began fidgeting now, beginning to worry that Grampa was going to preach, or something.

Gathering little Emma into his lap, Grampa continued with determination. "In fact, if those events had never happened, there would be no Christmas. I guess you could say Hanukkah saved Christmas."

Everyone was interested now.

"Rachel said something about a guy named Judas Maccabeus. She said that he cleansed the temple and that there was a miracle with the lamp oil. I really don't get it, Grampa. What's the big deal? Why was it so important?"

"Well, there is a whole lot more to the story than that, Matt, as you are realizing. This was a very terrible time for Israel. God had given them instructions about how they should live and conduct themselves. The most important thing was that they were to worship Him and Him only. Instead they followed the ways of the surrounding countries and began to worship and serve other gods - idols made of stone and wood. God had promised them great blessing and continual peace if they obeyed Him. Since they were disobedient they removed themselves from His protection.

At that same time there was a Syrian king named Antiochus the Fourth.."

"Wait a minute, wait a minute.." interrupted Nathan. "What kind of king named what?"...

"He was the king of Syria. Syria was a nearby nation that was Israel's enemy. Actually, it still is today. The king's name was Antiochus the Fourth."

"Who would name their baby Antiochus? Like, 'Here, Antiochus, come to dinner!'" Nathan was getting a little sidetracked.

"Tyler, can you say Anti – ochus?" asked Grampa, ignoring Nathan.

"Anti-ochus." Replied Tyler thoughtfully.

"Very good, let's continue with the story. Anyway, the Syrians hated the Jews and wanted the entire race to either give up their religion or be killed. As you know, God had given laws that the Jews were to live by, and one of those laws was that they should not eat pig meat or other animals that God had said were unclean. One of Antiochus' plans was to force Jews to eat pig. Antiochus wanted the Jews to worship Zeus, the Greek god. He even put a statue of Zeus in the Holy Temple in Jerusalem and defiled the holy altars by sacrificing pigs and other unclean animals to Zeus. He wanted to put a complete end to Judaism. You see, the Messiah was supposed to come from the Jews, and if the Jews were destroyed, the Messiah could not come, and the world would be without a savior. Antiochus the Fourth was actually fighting against God and His plan for mankind.

"What is 'Messiah' Grampa?" asked Matt.

"'Messiah' simply means 'The Anointed One'. You are more familiar with the word 'Christ.' The Greek word, Christ, means the same thing as the Hebrew word 'Messiah.'"

"I still don't understand..." Matt faltered as the rest of the family also listened intently to this story. Even the young ones were still by now. Baby Emma was happy to simply cuddle in Grampa's arms and suck her thumb.

"Mattathias, Judas' father, was a Priest of God." Grampa continued. "He was faithful to keep God's commandments. Antiochus' men tried to force him and his sons to eat pig meat that had been sacrificed to Zeus, hoping that their example would encourage the people to join in. Mattathias and his family refused to do what he said. They tore down the altar and fought back. Then they, and others who also loved God, ran out of the city and camped in the mountains. Judas gathered these men into a small army to fight the mighty Syrian army. All they had were a few men and almost no decent weapons, and yet they won the battle. How do you suppose they were able to do that?"

"God?" Matt answered.

"Yes, it was a miracle of God."

"Judas went back to the Temple and could not believe the destruction. Blood, ashes, dirt, and the remains of pigs covered the courts and holy place.   The Syrian armies had senselessly destroyed books and stolen furnishings. But, at least the temple was still there. The Maccabees, as Judas' army was called, had defeated the Syrians before they had completely destroyed everything. Remember, the Temple was a grand and awesome place! It was made with cedar and pure gold. The worship of the One True God and sacrifices to Him could not resume unless it was cleaned up and again sanctified.

"Matt, remember when Ryan threw the paint all over your table?"

"Yeah... It was a real mess."

"What did you have to do with the cookies?"

"I had to throw them away."

"Why?"

"Because they were ruined. They had paint all over them."

"Exactly. And dinner could not be served because the table was messed up. The cookies could not be eaten because they were defiled. They were dirty. The table was defiled because it had paint on it. You cleaned it up with cleaning cloths and soap. You cleaned until the paint was all gone. That is a good example of what took place in that Temple. Some things had to be thrown out because they were defiled. Other things could be saved by cleansing them properly.

"Like the dead rat defiled our porch?" Matt grimaced. He was still on this track.

"Yes, like that too. Your father had to take it out and bury it so it would not stink and draw other vermin.

"But there was also another real problem." Grampa continued the story. "There was only one day's worth of holy oil for the candlestick. God required that the candlestick should never go out. Your mom made more cookies and it probably took her about 45 minutes. Making holy oil for the Temple took a long time - days. When the Temple was clean and again sanctified to the Holy God of Heaven, they lit the candles and began making the new oil according to God's special recipe. One day's worth of oil burned for the entire eight days that it took to make more. They made a decree that all the people should celebrate the Dedication of the Temple for 8 days each year from then on. They celebrate this wonderful miracle today."

"What's a decree, Grampa?" asked Tyler.

"A decree is like a law," Grampa answered patiently.

Grampa then took the menorah and put the nine candles in it. He asked, "Do you see anything unusual about this candlestick? Remember, we are celebrating the fact that the oil burned for eight days."

"Yeah! Why nine candles?" Nathan asked curiously.

"Aha! You noticed! The ninth candle, the one that stands higher than the rest, is called the Shamas, or servant candle. All the other candles are lit by the Shamas. Why do you suppose they added this candle?"

"To represent God Who multiplied the oil?" Matt answered.

"Smart boy! And remember Jesus said that He was a servant King. He also told us to be servants. One way we serve is by bringing His light to the world."

"Jesus is also the Light of the world!" Matt was getting excited now. He was seeing something new.

"Yes, and this celebration is a beautiful picture of that very fact." Grampa added.

"Wow! He could have used that candlestick as an example of Who He was!"

"I think you've got it." Grampa said meaningfully.

"But how did this all save Christmas? I mean, I do see now how important it all was, but I still don't see the connection."

"Well, our enemy, the devil, understood that if the Jewish people were destroyed, the Messiah could not come..."

"...And Jesus was a Jew!"

"That's right. The promised Messiah, the Savior of the whole earth, had to come through the Jewish people because that is what God said would happen. God had also said through the prophets that the Messiah would go into the Holy Temple. If the Temple had been destroyed...."

"Then that couldn't have happened either!" Matt interrupted excitedly.

"Yes, Matt. Everything God says, He will do. Many things God said would happen about Jesus took place in that Temple. Simeon recognized Jesus as a baby. Jesus confounded the Rabbis when He was only twelve years old. He healed people. He spoke of Himself and taught those who would listen."

Grampa lit the shamas candle and let each one light a candle with it.

Everyone looked into the light as though they had never seen a candle before. Each one worshipped God silently in his heart.

"I can't wait to see Rachel. I understand now how important Hanukkah is. I probably need to apologize to her, too. I was kind of mean to her. We wouldn't have ever had a chance to know God in the first place if it wasn't for the Jews." Matt was full. Full of appreciation for God, for his family, for this very special Christmas, and for the things he had learned.

Chapter Nine

Homecoming

Rachel and Matt wandered through the city park near their neighborhood. Matt had returned home the night before, and Rachel was very happy to see him. It had been a lonely week for her.

"Rachel, I'm sorry."

"For what?"

"I was mean about Hanukkah. I really made fun of it."

"It's okay, Matt."

"No, it's not okay. Grampa explained to me what Hanukkah is and that we wouldn't even HAVE Christmas if Hanukkah hadn't happened."

"I don't get that..." Rachel said hesitantly.

"Well, it's a long story, but we Christians owe a lot to your people. We would never have known God without the Jewish people. Jesus was a Jew, you know."

"Yeah, I guess He was. I never really thought of it that way." Rachel still didn't exactly understand the change of attitude in her friend. She had never heard a Christian talk like this before. They always seemed so know-it-all. So smug or something. Like they were better than her. Although Matt was her best friend, even he acted like that sometimes. And she had never considered that Jews and Christians might have something in common. This was new. This was nice. She definitely liked the change. And she was becoming curious. She added, "Well, ...maybe I should learn a little more about Christmas..."